W9-BZA-812

DISCARD

# The Rain

# The Rain

By MICHAEL LASER

Illustrated by JEFFREY GREENE

SIMON & SCHUSTER BOOKS FOR YOUNG READERS

E

SIMON & SCHUSTER BOOKS FOR YOUNG READERS

An imprint of Simon & Schuster Children's Publishing Division

1230 Avenue of the Americas

New York, New York 10020

SIMON & SCHUSTER BOOKS FOR YOUNG READERS is a trademark of Simon & Schuster.

Book design by Lucille Chomowicz

The text of this book is set in Hiroshige Book

The illustrations are rendered in pastels

Printed and bound in the United States of America

First Edition

10 9 8 7 6 5 4 3 2 1

Library of Congress Cataloging-in-Publication Data

Laser, Michael.

The rain / by Michael Laser ; illustrated by Jeffrey Greene.

p.          cm.

Summary: In the city, the town, and the forest, people enjoy
the beauty of a gentle autumn rainfall.

[1. Rain and rainfall—Fiction.] I. Greene, Jeffrey, ill. II. Title.

PZ7.L32717Rai   1997   [E]—dc20   96-34179   CIP   AC

ISBN 0-689-80506-3

For Helen
—M. L.


For Rick, Louise, Ron, Janet, Doug, Brian,
Stephanie, and Laura
—J. G.

The rain fell on the city, the town, and the forest.

In the city, the rain fell on thousands of people at the same time. Some had umbrellas, some put newspapers over their heads, and some ran into doorways to stay dry. A tall man in a green raincoat bought an umbrella outside a train station.

In the town, the rain fell quietly on the houses and streets. It made such a peaceful sound that a teacher fell asleep by her window as she read her students' homework.

Just outside the town, a girl and boy explored the forest. The rain pattered on the leaves high above them. Only a few drops reached them through the leaves—just enough to wet their hair.

"Where does rain come from?" the boy asked his sister, who was older.

She knew about clouds, but she said,
"It comes from the moon."

The boy didn't believe her. He threw a pinecone straight up into the air and said, "Umbrellas on the moon!"

The man in the green raincoat looked out the window of the train. Far away the city buildings looked gray and misty. Droplets moved in shivering streaks across the window.

Looking down at the street, he saw an old man smile up into the falling raindrops. The old man had no umbrella, but he didn't seem to care.

Why was the old man smiling? Because he had taken off his glasses, which were spotty with drops, and now the whole world looked like bright, blurry colors to him. The traffic light was bright green, the lights on the backs of the cars were bright red, and the neon sign in the shoe store window was bright blue. Everything looked so different without his glasses— it was like discovering a new world.

In the quiet town, the rain came through the open window and touched the teacher's arm. Waking up, she saw the rain falling straight down on the green grass.

The yellow house across the street looked so pretty, with the wet flowers in front and the rain bouncing off the walk, that she wanted to preserve it. Although she hadn't painted a picture in many years, she took her old watercolors out to the porch and set to work.

Just then the boy and girl came to the edge of the forest. A wide field separated the forest from the town. A crow flew over the field, its black feathers wet and glistening.

They decided not to wait for the rain to stop. Walking home, they paused to watch the raindrops make tiny splashes in a pond. Each drop made its own *plunk*.

The boy wondered if baby fish lived in the raindrops. He held his hands out to catch the rain but couldn't find any fish.

While the train sped toward his town, the man in the raincoat thought about the day long ago when he had waited in the forest for the rain to stop. The sun had gone down, and so he had walked home in the dark, with the raindrops falling on his face and hair and hands.

The darkness had scared him. But when he got home and told his family about the walk in the night rain, it seemed like an adventure.

He had forgotten that day until the old man's smile reminded him.

Out in the field, the sister and brother were so wet that their clothes stuck to them and their hair straggled down in front of their eyes. "You look funny," the girl said.

"No, you," the boy answered.

They turned it into a song, "No you, no you, no you, no you."

They took their muddy shoes off and washed them in a stream at the edge of the woods before they went home.

The man in the green raincoat opened his new umbrella when he got off the train. Seeing that no one else was around, he tipped the umbrella to the side and let the rain fall on his face. The drops on his lips made him smile.

He found his wife on the porch finishing a watercolor painting of a yellow house. She pointed down the street to their children running home and singing, "Rain, rain, rain, rain."

Instead of hurrying her son and daughter inside to dry off, the mother asked, "What was it like in the forest in the rain?"

The girl said, "You could hear it falling on the leaves, high up."

"We saw a crow," the boy said.

They left their shoes on the porch and went inside. The father told them about the old man smiling into the rain, and about the night when he walked home in the rain and dark.

Back in the city, the old man was eating a bowl of soup at his table. He could still hear the rain through the open window. No matter what happens in the world, he thought, the rain still makes a beautiful sound.

Later, when they were all asleep, the rain became softer . . . and softer . . . and then it stopped.

E
L          Laser, Michael
098-280PTO      The Rain

| DATE DUE | | | |
|---|---|---|---|
|  |  |  |  |
|  |  |  |  |
|  |  |  |  |
|  |  |  |  |
|  |  |  |  |
|  |  |  |  |
|  |  |  |  |
|  |  |  |  |
|  |  |  |  |
|  |  |  |  |
|  |  |  |  |
|  |  |  |  |
|  |  |  |  |

R.L. 4.2